First published in the United States, Great Britain, Canada, Australia, and New Zealand
in 2009 by North-South Books, an imprint of NordSüd Verlag AG, CH-8005 Zürich, Switzerland.
Distributed in the United States by North-South Books Inc., New York 10001.

Library of Congress Cataloging-in-Publication Data is available.
ISBN: 978-0-7358-2202-3 (trade edition).
2 4 6 8 10 – 9 7 5 3
Printed in USA.

www.northsouth.com

Christoph Schuler
Rahel Nicole Eisenring

Kiki

NorthSouth
New York / London

Early one morning in the spring,
Kiki hatched.
"Hello!" she cheeped. "I'm here!"
But not a single hen in the henhouse
paid any attention.

The hens were too busy arguing.
"White eggs are best!"
"Brown eggs are better!"
"White!" "Brown!" "White!" "Brown!" squawked the hens.
"Cheep?" said Kiki. "Hello?"

At last Mother Hen noticed her new chick.
"Kiki!" she cried. "My lovely egg has hatched at last!"
Then she went right back to arguing.
"White!" "Brown!" "White!" "Brown!"

All the noise in the henhouse brought Farmer Bill on the run.

"What's all this fuss?" he cried. "You're disturbing my nap! Keep this up and, rest assured, a bad end will come of it!"

The hens fluttered off in all directions.

"Oh, dear," thought Kiki. "I don't know if I'm going to like it here!"

No sooner did Farmer Bill leave the henhouse than a weasel slipped in.

"Good morning, dear ladies," said the weasel. "I couldn't help but hear you arguing. I have had some experience with eggs. Allow me to inspect your eggs and be the judge."

"Oh!" exclaimed the hens. "An egg expert!" They carefully dusted their eggs and lined them up for inspection.

But something did not look quite right to Kiki. With an egg in his mouth, the weasel was backing toward the door.

Kiki jumped up and down. She whistled. She flapped her small wings.

"Do something!" she shouted. "The weasel is stealing your eggs!"

But the hens didn't hear her. They were back to squabbling.

"Brown!" "White!" "Brown!" "White!"

Before long, every egg thief in the neighborhood got the news:
The hens were too busy quarreling to watch their eggs. New thieves
appeared every day to carry or roll or fly off with an egg. The only
one who seemed to notice was Kiki.

Then one day, Kiki met a rabbit stretched out in the grass.

Rabbit did not want to steal eggs. He just wanted to be friends. Kiki told him all her troubles.

"The hens are so busy arguing, they pay no attention to their eggs," she cheeped sadly.

"Hmm," said Rabbit. "I have an idea. Listen carefully." And Rabbit whispered in Kiki's ear.

That night, while Rabbit sat outside keeping
watch, Kiki went to work.

The next morning, the hens awoke to find
all their eggs painted red and yellow and green
and blue, with stripes and polka dots and even
little hearts.

"What have you *done?*"
they squawked at Kiki.

"Look at our eggs!"

"What about *brown?*"

"What about *white?*"

The noise in the henhouse woke Farmer Bill.

"More squawking!" he grumbled. "Maybe I'll put you all in the soup pot!"

Then he caught sight of the brightly painted eggs.

"Ho-ho!" he cried. "What clever chickens! And just in time for Easter! Everyone will love these beautiful eggs!"

For once, the hens had nothing to say.

And that is how peace came to the henhouse.

Now the chickens lay their eggs, Kiki paints them, and Rabbit delivers them in a wicker basket.

Farmer Bill is doing so well, he bought some new boots for himself and a portable TV for the henhouse.

And the hens never argue anymore about whose egg is the most beautiful. Well, almost never.